Tessa Moore

Illustrated by Terry Myler

THE CHILDREN'S PRESS

To Dan,
the original bear

First published 2002 by
The Children's Press
an imprint of Anvil Books
45 Palmerston Road, Dublin 6

2 4 6 8 7 5 3 1

© Text Tessa Moore 2002
© Illustrations Terry Myler 2002
© Poem *Under a Chair* and illustration Brendan O'Reilly 2002

ISBN 1 901737 43 8

Typeset by Computertype Limited
Printed by Colour Books Limited

J/4, 33/
€5. 25

Contents

1 Flash Fox

Flash Fox was a very smart fox.

He was the smartest fox in the whole forest.

Anything he wore was IN. Anything he didn't wear was OUT.

That was why he was known as Flash Fox.

The Fox family had owned
the Corner Shop for ages.

As it was the only shop for
miles around – except for a
grotty Fast Food joint – every-
one had to shop there.

So the Foxes became very
rich.

Once life was very pleasant
for Flash Fox. He got up late,
had a hot bath, then came down
for coffee and rolls, all just
made by his doting ma.

At noon he strolled through the forest to the shop, where Old Squirrel made him a cup of coffee and told him how much money he had made the day before.

He would dip into the till for some of it and go to the Club. There he would have lunch with his rich friends.

Afterwards, he would read the papers and have a little snooze. Another visit to the shop and then home.

There he would fling himself into a great big armchair and say, with a yawn, 'I'm flat out from all the work.'

And Ma would say, as they ate their four-course dinner, 'You work too hard. Get rid of that old fool of a squirrel. You're paying *him* and *you're* doing all the work.'

And Flash Fox would say, 'Ma, I can't. He's family.'

The *real* reason was that Old Squirrel made money for him.

He bought things called 'shares' and sold them for a profit. But Ma said this was gambling so Flash Fox never told her about it.

'Family! Just because he's a third cousin, twice removed.'

She had no idea what 'twice removed' meant but it sounded very grand.

2 Disaster

In due course, and at a ripe old age, Old Squirrel left for the Great Nuttery in the sky.

'Now,' said Ma Fox, 'you'll be able to get in a smart young fox and you won't have to work so hard.'

'I will,' promised Flash Fox.

But that was before he had a look at the books.

He nearly died of fright.

Nothing but bills. Money was owing all over the place.

But where was all the money Old Squirrel told him he had made? All those profits!

He went to Old Squirrel's house and looked everywhere.

Under the bed. In the attic.

He took the bathroom apart.

There wasn't sight or sound of the money *anywhere*. It had vanished!

Then he found a diary. It began: 'Today I bought a lot of shares in a new company. I'm

told the money will double in a
year's time. My master will be
so pleased!

'*And there is no risk!*'

The last entry read: 'Alas,
disaster! The shares are now
worth much less than what I
paid for them. The money is
gone. What will I do...?'

'Well, we know what he did,'
said Ma Fox. 'He up and died.
That was a big help. *Gambling!*
And with *your* money! I told
you to get rid of him.'

'I trusted him,' said Flash
Fox.

'More fool you. Now, what are you going to do?'

Flash Fox thought for a while. Then he had a great idea.

He would run the shop himself! It couldn't be all that hard. If Old Squirrel could do it, surely he, who had far more brains, could do it better!

He would make lots of
money. Then he would open
another shop. And another. *Then*
he could hire lots of staff

But he didn't like the work at
all. It was very tiring.

He had to stand on his feet all day, at the beck and call of stupid shoppers who came in for a little bit of this and a little bit of that.

Half the time they didn't know what they wanted, so they kept changing their minds.

And they were so easily put off buying anything at all.

Those who *did* buy anything went on and on about the high prices and the poor quality and things being out of stock.

But what really drove him wild was to overhear people talking about him.

Loudly. As if he wasn't there.

'Well, I never thought I'd see the day when Flash Fox was serving in his own shop. What a comedown!'

'Poor chap, he must have fallen on hard times.'

When Ma Fox got the first
week's takings, she blew up.

'Is this all you made last
week? I can't live on that. What
about my skiing holiday? New
car? Hairdos? Parties?'

'It's not easy,' said Flash.

'You're worse than that old fool of a squirrel. You're not cut out for this work. Get yourself a good sharp manager.'

'We can't afford it.'

'It won't cost anything if you get the right chap – it will *pay*.'

So he let it be known at the
Club that he wanted a manager.

A brash young wolf came in,
looked around the shop and said,
'What a dump! Needs a face lift.
A *drastic* face lift!'

He took out his mobile phone, snapped it on and said: 'Memo to myself. Get in touch with Design Inc... wanted design new super-shop... state-of the art... money no object...'

He snapped off his mobile. 'Now... about salary...'

He named a figure which made Flash Fox feel faint.

Then he went on, 'Share options, of course...'

Flash Fox, who had never heard of share options, said faintly, 'Of course.'

'Company car. Bonus every six months. Expenses. Two months' holiday....'

His mobile rang. 'Yup... on the way... see you in zing time.'

He shot out, saying, 'Don't call me, FF, I'll call you.' He left the door open behind him.

Flash Fox went home in a
raging humour.

'How did it go?' asked Ma.

'No go. All they want now is
money. No one wants to work!'

'Why not get a bear?'

'A bear?'

'They're great workers and
take low wages.'

GET A BEAR!

'I thought bears were stupid.'

'Of course they are. Why else do you think they work hard for very little? Now, put this ad in the paper.'

The ad read:

SMART BEAR WANTED

ALL DUTIES

GOOD WAGES
FOR THE RIGHT BEAR

APPLY: THE CORNER SHOP

3 Bono

In another part of the forest,
Ma Bear was trying to clean the
house.

Her son was jigging around to
music. He was singing:

I once met a bear,
*   With a flower in his hair.*
When I started to stare,
*   He gave such a glare.*

'Call that a song?' Ma shouted at him.

'Ma, there aren't songs any more.'

'What are they now?'

'They're about life. Real life. The poor, the weak...'

Ma rolled her eyes.

'Listen, son. I'm telling you for the last time. You'll never make a pop star.'

'Ma, I have a good voice.'

'Says who? Changing your name to Bono – what was wrong with Bertie, anyway? – and sticking an earring in your ear isn't going to make you into a pop star. Give up!'

'What do you want me to do, Ma?'

'Get yourself a job. Work! We need the dosh.'

Just then the clock on the wall struck twelve.

Bono gave a great big smile, 'What's for dinner?'

Ma whipped the cover off a large plate.

There was nothing on it.

Bono stared at it for a long time.

'What's the story?' he asked at last.

'No money, no honey... that's the story. Here, take this...' she pushed a rusk into one paw and

a piece of paper into the other
'... and this. Answer it at once!'

Bono Bear looked at it while
he was eating his rusk which
was very, very dry.

SMART BEAR WANTED
ALL DUTIES
GOOD WAGES
FOR THE RIGHT BEAR
APPLY: THE CORNER SHOP

'Smart bear? I wouldn't be
able for that. I'm not smart.'

'You're as smart as that fool
of a fox. Go now, before anyone
else gets there.'

37

As Bono finished his rusk, he said, 'Ma, I've just thought of a new song. You'll like it. It's about the Unequal Distribution of Wealth.'

The cupboard is bare,
Which just isn't fair.
Why is it a bear,
Doesn't get a fair share?

'Out!' growled Ma Bear. 'Never mind about the distribution of wealth. Get out and get some.

'And whatever you do, don't burst into song. And keep that earring hidden.'

4 The Test

As Bono strolled through the
forest he was sniffing the
flowers and singing.

A cat passed by and Bono
sang to her:

You're a cute little cat,
  There's no doubt about that.
But what are you at?
  In that horrible hat.

At the Corner Shop, Flash
Fox had cleared a space and set
up a desk.

'Name?' he asked Bono.

'Bono.'

'That's not a real name. I
mean the one you were born
with.'

'I had no name when I was
born.'

'Don't quibble,' scowled
Flash Fox. 'I mean what were
you called before you called
yourself Bono.'

'Bertie... Bertie Bear.'

'Now, Bertie, are you a smart
bear?'

'Yes,' said Bono, putting his
arm up to hide his earring.

'Looks pretty thick to me,' thought Flash to himself.

'That fox is a fool,' thought Bono to himself.

'I'm going to give you some simple sums. Are you ready.'

'Sure, fire away.'

'Addition first. What's: *one-and-one-and-one-and-one-and-one-and-one-and-one-and-one-and-one-and-one-and-one.*'

'Ten,' said Bono.

Flash Fox was amazed.

'Are you sure? You must have lost count.'

'*I* didn't... I think *you did.*'

'Let's see if you can subtract,' said Flash Fox hastily. 'Take 10 away from 8.'

Bono looked puzzled.

'I think he's trying to work it out!' thought Flash Fox to himself. 'He's too stupid to know there *isn't* an answer! Ma was right about bears.'

Bono took out a pencil and began to write on a pad he had taken from his pocket.

'You can add nothing to the 8,' said Flash.

'Thanks,' said Bono, making a note. 'The answer is 70.'

'That's impossible. Show me that pad.'

Bono held it up.

'But I said you couldn't add anything to the 8.'

47

'You didn't. You said I could add *nothing*. Nothing is nought. 'So I added that to the 8 and made 80. Then I took away 10. Answer – 70. Q.E.D.'

'Q.E.D?'

'Quite easily done.'

'Can you multiply?' scowled Flash Fox.

'Of course!'

'Multiply 236 by 548.'

'129,328.'

'How did you do that?'

'I used my calculator.'

'But you're not allowed to use a calculator.'

'But you didn't say that, did you?' said Bono with a yawn. 'About a calculator.

'Do you really want someone stupid enough to multiply 236 x 548 the old long way when it can be done in a flash? That would be stupid of *you*.'

Flash Fox was getting cross.
'Let's see if you can divide,'
he snarled.

He took the lid off a big jar of
sweets and spilled them on to
the table.

'Honey drops,' thought Bono.
'My most favourite sweet!'

'Divide this pile into two
parts. I'll give you ten seconds.
Starting from now.'

He looked at his watch.

When he looked up, there
were two piles on the table.
There were two sweets in front
of him. The rest were in front of
Bono.

'That isn't two equal piles.'

'But you didn't say two *equal* piles, did you? You just said two piles… and there they are. Two piles.'

He scooped up his and put them into a paper bag.

'Now, when do I start?' asked
Bono

'Not so fast. We have to
decide on your wages. You will
get one jar of honey a week.'

'I need at least two.'

'Well, that's the offer. Take it
or leave it.'

Bono had got up and was
wandering around.

'Now, what's he up to?'
thought Flash. 'Never met such
a daft animal in all my life.
I sure don't want him here. He'd
drive me mad in five seconds.
I'll tell him to go.'

Just then the fire alarm bell sounded.

'Fire! Fire! Fire!' screamed Flash Fox, rushing for the door.

As soon as he got outside, the door was slammed shut behind him.

HA, HA, HE, HE

Bono Bear was grinning at him from *inside* the shop.

He had set off the alarm.

'Let me in,' shouted Flash. 'I'll report you to the police. That's a Criminal Offence, setting off an alarm. They'll put you in prison.'

'I don't think so,' said Bono. 'What are you going to tell them?

'You're going to look a bit silly if you say you were locked out of your own shop by a stupid bear. They may think that *you* were the stupid one!'

FLASH FOX
TRICKED
OUT OF SHOP

Flash Fox was raging mad.

'Joke's gone on long enough,' he growled. 'Let me in.'

'I have the job? At three jars of honey a week?'

'You said two.'

'Ah, that was then. This is now. Well, make up your mind. I can't stand around all day. I've other things to do.'

5 End Game

That was how Bono Bear got the better of Flash Fox. But it's not the end of the story.

When the door was opened and Flash Fox got in again, he found Bono Bear sitting in his chair.

'We've a few things to talk about,' said Bono.

'Like what?'

'The name. The Corner Shop. That's out of the ark. What about this?'

He pushed his pad over to Flash Fox. On it was written:

'Why not Fox and Bear?'

'Well, if you insist.'

Bono Bear put out a paw.

'I think this is the start of a beautiful friendship.'

As Bono walked home, he was humming to himself.

I'm a very smart bear,
 With grey cells to spare.
So it's really quite fair,
 That I get a half share!

'How did it go?' asked Ma Fox.

'You were wrong,' said Flash,
'bears are very, very smart.'

'How did it go?' asked Ma
Bear.

'I think we're in business,'
said Bono.

CHIMP CHAT

This fine-looking fellow is an orang-utan. The name literally means *man (orang) **of the forest** (utan)*. He comes from the islands of Borneo and Sumatra in southern Asia (south of China and east of India) and as you can guess he lives in the forests, up among the tree-tops. He's about two-thirds the size of a gorilla but bigger than a chimp.